[redacted]

Doodle Dog

in Space

Eric Seltzer

ALADDIN PAPERBACKS
New York London Toronto Sydney

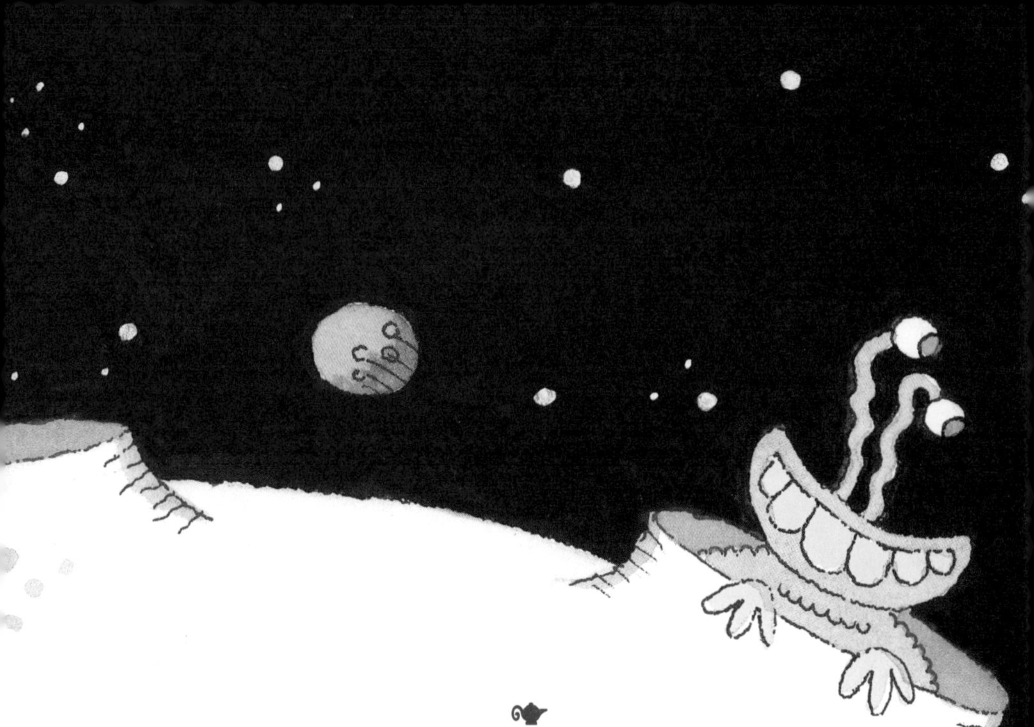

ALADDIN PAPERBACKS
An imprint of Simon & Schuster Children's Publishing Division
1230 Avenue of the Americas, New York, NY 10020

Designed by Lisa Vega
The text of this book was set in CenturyOldst BT.
Manufactured in the United States of America
First Aladdin Paperbacks edition December 2005
2 4 6 8 10 9 7 5 3 1
Library of Congress Cataloging-in-Publication Data
Seltzer, Eric.
Doodle Dog in space / by Eric Seltzer.
p. cm.
Summary: An artistic dog and his friend share adventures in space.
ISBN-13: 978-0-689-85912-0
ISBN-10: 0-689-85912-0
[1. Dogs—Fiction. 2. Space flight—Fiction. 3. Art—Fiction.
4. Solar system—Fiction. 5. Stories in rhyme.] I. Title.
PZ8.3.S4665Dr 2005
[E]—dc22 2003027330

For Jennifer Weiss,
my trusty editor

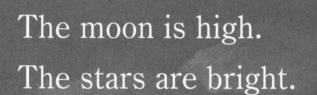

The moon is high.
The stars are bright.

The sky calls out
to us tonight.

I pack my bone.

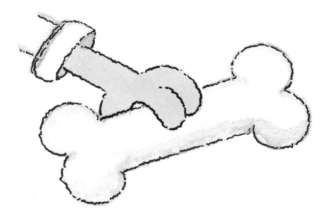

King gets some clay.

We both will fly

to space today.

I get out
my Doodle Kit.

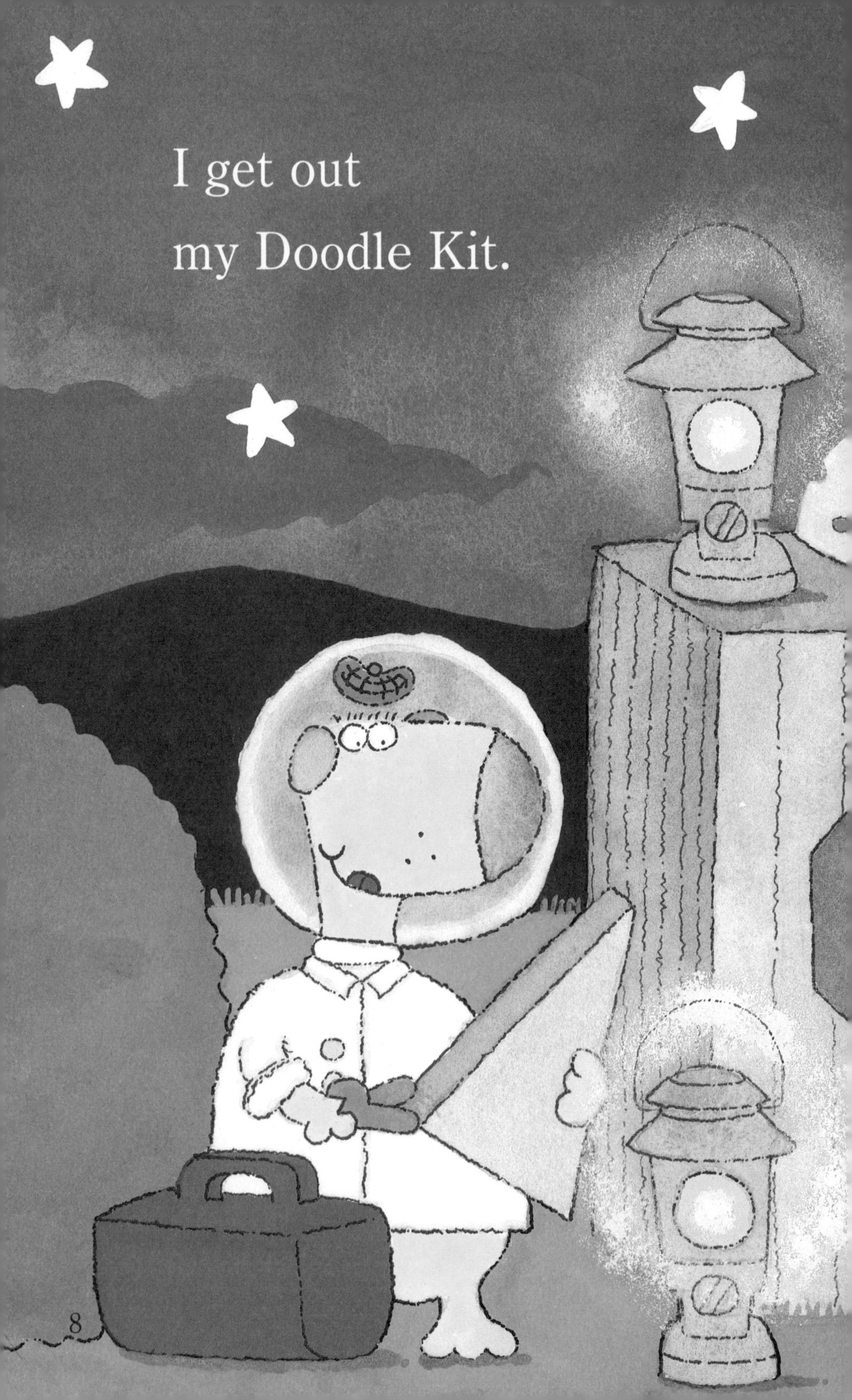

We cut and paste
a rocket ship.

Blasting off
on 3-2-1,

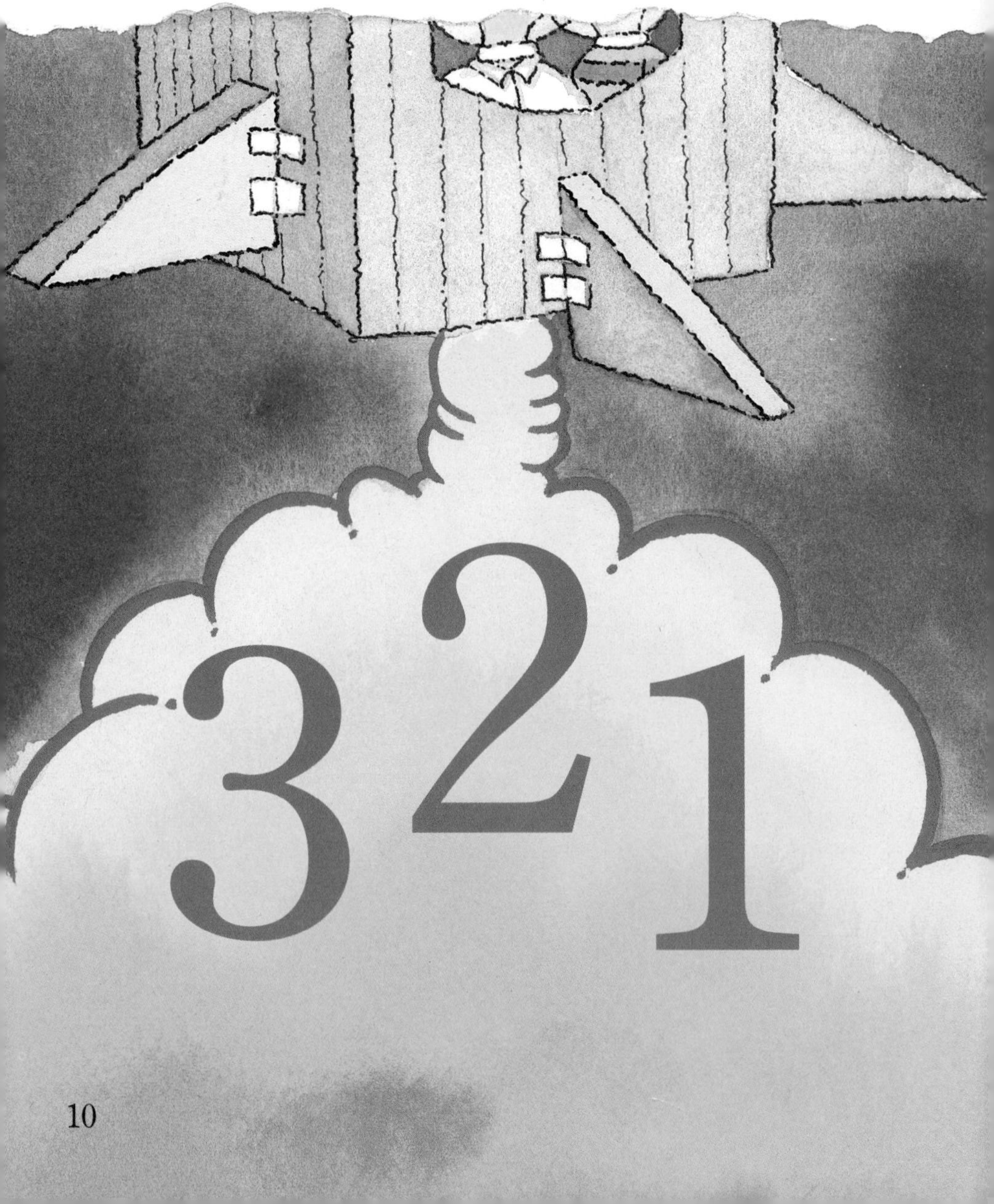
3 2 1

for a trip
around the sun!

I get a map
and drive to Mars.

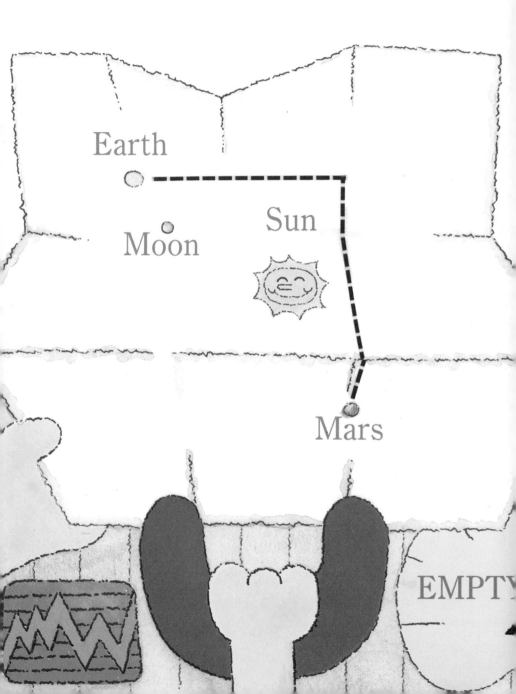

Earth

Moon

Sun

Mars

EMPTY

We slip and slide
on shooting stars.

On Mars our space pals
give us lunch—

lots of fries
and lots of punch.

With space pop
we bunny hop.

With space ma
we cha-cha-cha.

It is noon.
Time to fly!

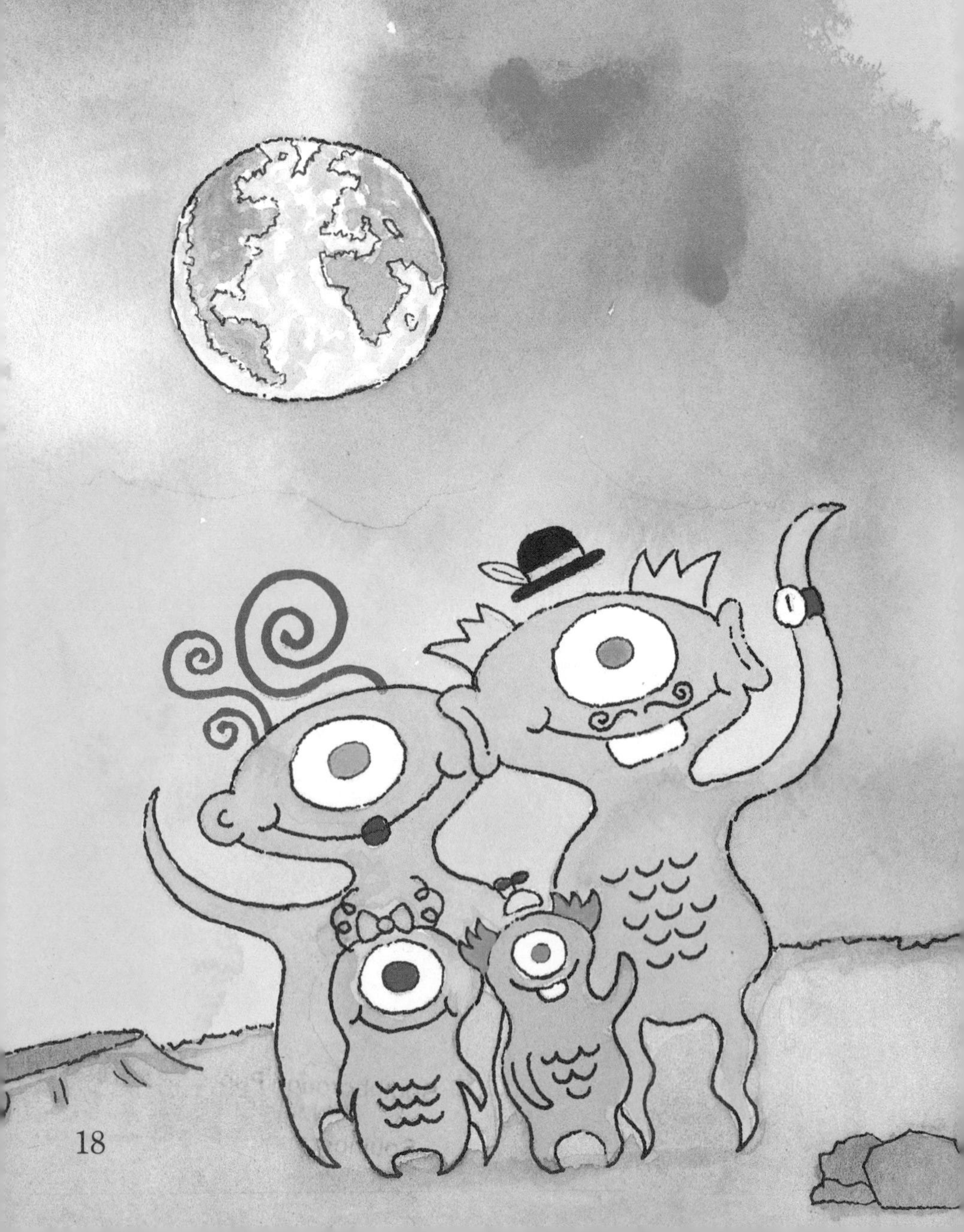

We say, "Thanks,"
and wave good-bye.

As we leave
we hear a thump.

Falling rocks!
We bounce and bump.

King and I
cry out, "Mayday!"

MAYDAY!

We crash on
the Milky Way.

I take a pin
to fix a fin.

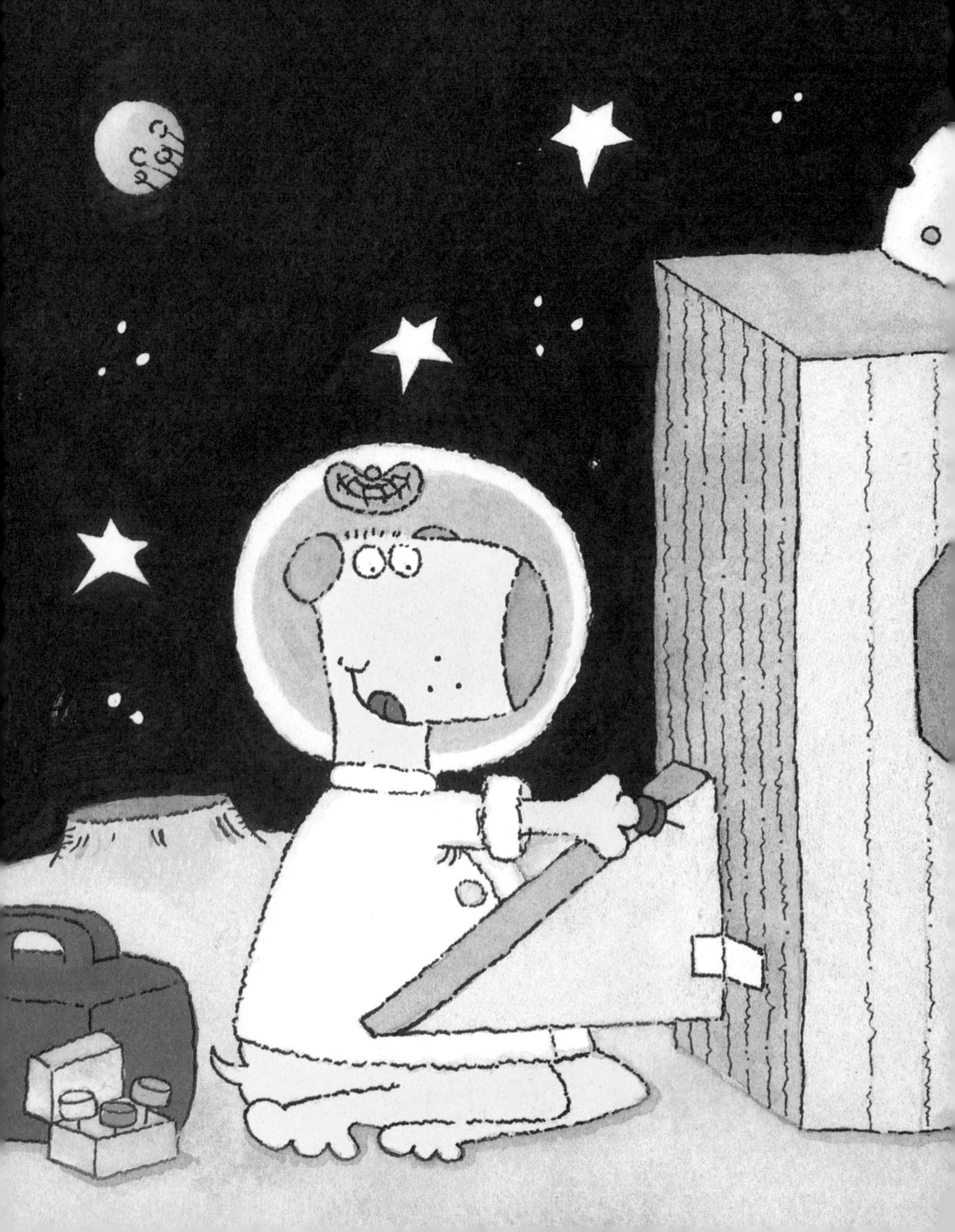

King takes a bone
to patch the cone.

Next we hear
a clink and clank.

What was that?
An empty tank!

ALERT

EMPTY

FULL

It looks like
the gas is low.

SPACE
GAS AND GO

Fill her up
and go, go, go!

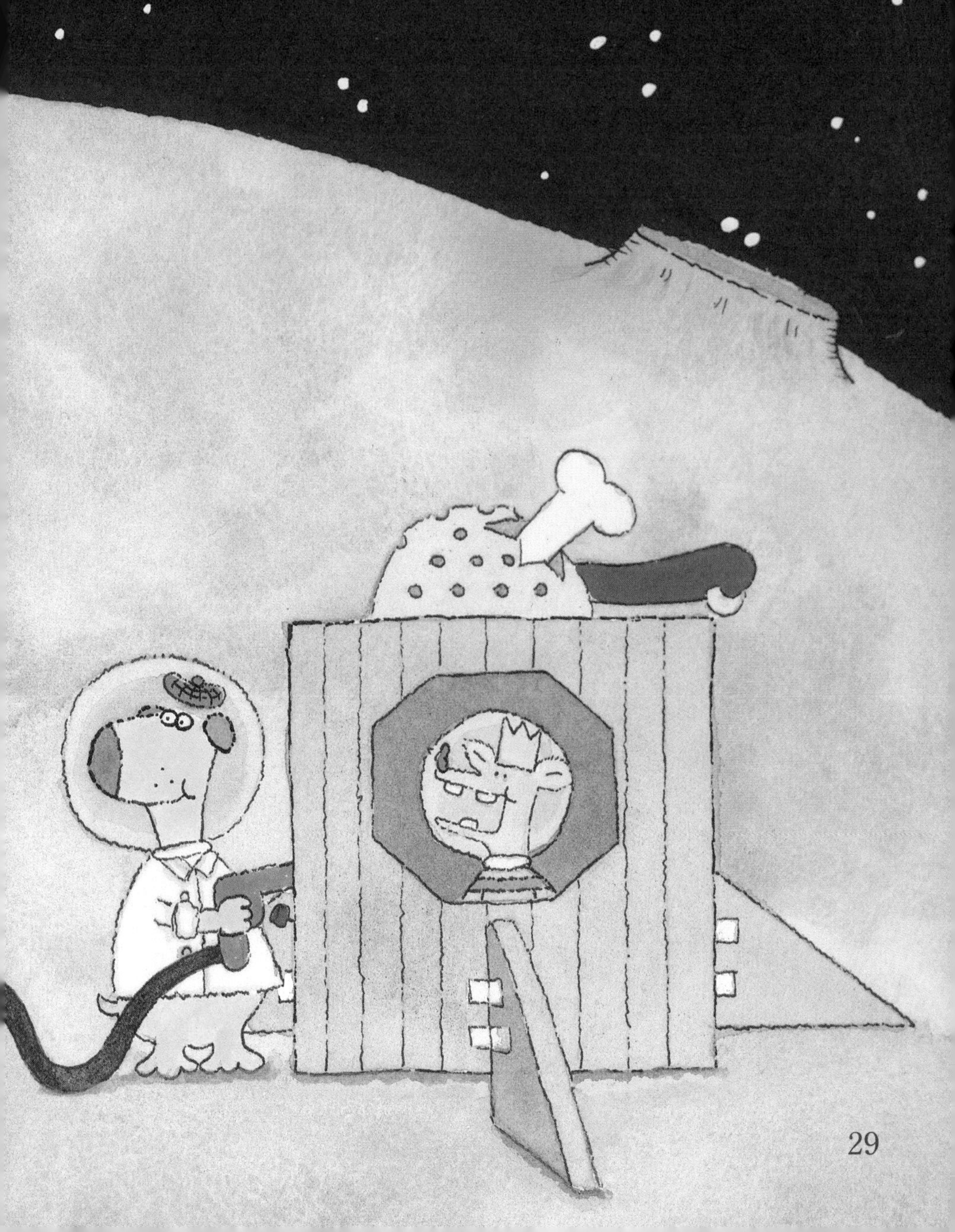

I grab my pad
and draw a star—

first, so close,
then so far.

As we land
King sings out,
"Stars and moon,
over and out!"